Caleb Finds A Friend

by
Paul Hart
COVER DESIGN BY
Scott Hall

15678

ISBN – 1-885101-05-8

Writer's Press Service
Boise, Idaho

I dedicate "Caleb" to my mother and father because this is my first children's book.

I dedicate "Caleb" to my wife Peg and our kids; Lucy, Sam and Sarah, because they love books... "**SAM!!!** – take that book out of your mouth! (Yucky) ... sheesh."

I dedicate "Caleb" to Mr. and Mrs. "C" because they showed me how to reach.

I dedicate "Caleb" to Scott Hall because of a **GREAT** cover design even when he was very busy – Thanks!

I dedicate "Caleb" to all those who inspired me to dream, and for you Yogi, for making those dreams come true.

Last – but not least, I dedicate "Caleb" to my little buddy, Caleb ... because ... because ... just because!
HAPPY BIRTHDAY!

When Grandpa Storyteller isn't fishing or golfing, he loves to read books.

Most of all, he loves to tell his grandchildren stories.

When his grandchildren come over for a
visit, they run to him and ask, "Will you tell us
a story grandpa...Please?"

Grandpa always smiles and nods his head. First, Grandpa Storyteller settles into his chair as the kids gather.

"O.K. Grandpa, we're ready"
they shout.

"This story is about a little koala bear named Caleb who is looking for a friend."

"I like koala bears," said Mary Rose.

"So do I," smiled Grandpa Storyteller, then he continued.

Once upon a time . . .

. . . in a place where koala bears play,
lived a koala bear named Caleb.
It was Caleb's first birthday!

"Whatcha doin' Mom?"
"I'm baking a cake for your birthday," she said.
"What's a birthday?" asked Caleb.
He was not sure what a birthday was.

"You were born one year ago today," said Caleb's mom. "You can have anything you want."

"**ANYTHING?**"asked Caleb as birthday wishes raced through his head.

"Can I have a pair of scissors?"
"NO!" said Caleb's mom.
"Can I have the T.V. remote thingy?"
"NO!" she said again.
"Then I want a new friend," he said, and off he charged, almost running over dad.

Caleb began his search in the back yard. He always found the neatest stuff there. Sometimes he found big fat worms and shiny rocks. So, he was sure he could find a friend there as well.

"Maybe there's a friend under all of this
dirt!" he thought, as he started digging with
his daddy's shovel.

Minutes later, along came a big poofy
panda bear. "Whatcha doin' there, little guy?"
he asked.

"I'm looking for a friend!" said Caleb.

"Well HERE I AM!" announced the big poofy panda bear.

"GREAT!" said Caleb,
"You can help me look."

So, panda and Caleb began their search.

They looked up in the trees.

They looked down through the
basement window.

They looked in all of the bushes.

They even looked out over the fence
and down the street, but no friend could
be found.

"Maybe," said the panda, "it might help
if we knew what a friend was and what one
looked like."

"You're right!" said Caleb.
"C'mon ! Let's go ask Dad. He knows everything."

So off they ran into the house.

"Dad," said Caleb, "whats a friend?"

"A friend," said Dad, "a friend is some-one who knows all about you, but likes you anyway."

"HAHA HAHA HA."

"What does that mean?" whispered
panda.

"I think it means dad needs a friend
too," said Caleb.

Next, they went to ask Caleb's mom.
"Mom, what does a friend look like?"

"Oh, I think a friend looks like a big, poofy panda bear," said Caleb's mom with a grin.

"A panda bear?" asked Caleb.
"That sounds familiar," said panda.
"Didn't we see one of those in the back yard?"

"Yahoooo!" shouted panda
"OUT TO THE BACK YARD!" they yelled,
and off they ran.

They came to a puddle of water and saw their reflections.

"Hey, isn't that a panda?" asked Caleb.

"That looks like me," said panda.
Panda leaned over to see and his nose touched the water.

"That is me!" he said.

"Then **YOU** must be my friend!"

"I'm so glad!" declared panda.
"Me too," said Caleb.
And they gave each other a GREAT BIG
BEAR HUG.

Later, Caleb's mom had a birthday party for Caleb. Panda bear stayed to help celebrate.

Caleb couldn't take his eyes off of the candle.

Panda couldn't take his eyes off the birthday cake!

Caleb's birthday wish had come true: he had found a new friend. Caleb and panda ate lots of cake.

Birthday cake is one of panda's favorite foods. How do you think he got so POOFY?

"Sometimes we look very hard for the things we already have," said grandpa. Caleb looked and looked for a friend, when his friend panda was there helping him all the time.

THE END

"That was a good story Grandpa!"